D1685110

THE *First* CHRISTMAS GIFT

BRENTON YORGASON *and* KEVIN LUND

Bookcraft
Salt Lake City, Utah

We gratefully dedicate this book to our parents,
who taught us in our youth to think of Christ
and to strive to be like him.
We would also like to dedicate this story to the real Luke,
whose Christmas gift to Kevin inspired this story.

ISBN 0–88494–814–5

Fifth Printing, 1995

Printed in the United States of America

PART ONE

The Doing

I remember that day as if it were yesterday. And even though I was but a child of ten years, in my mind I was very grown up.

It began in the late afternoon of that memorable day, during the brief hour when the breeze begins and the air cools down. Well do I remember my hurried pace, as I attempted to complete my tasks and get into my father's home, without taking too much dust into my raspy, heaving chest. My eyes stung with newly acquired sand particles, and for just a moment I lamented my task of having to care for the two goats that stood secured to the post at the rear of our dwelling.

"Goat's milk," I muttered. "If only Mother were here, she could milk these smelly goats, and leave my time free in the early evenings—free to be in the hills, herding sheep with Father."

I squinted as I looked at the goats, who by this time were devouring the small bundle of grass I had placed before them. "Still, I love to drink your milk," I continued, speaking now directly to the beasts, somehow expecting them to understand my words. "And Father will be pleased to see how well I have cared for you both during his absence."

"Luke! Luke, please hurry! The bread is broken, and I'm *starved* . . ."

I gazed toward the door, feeling both frustration with and pride in my seven-year-old sister's impatience, knowing that my main charge was to care for her.

"Mary, my little one," I called, "close that door, or we'll be blessed with sand to eat, along with our evening bread. I'll be but a moment, and then we'll enjoy the best goat's milk in all of Judea!"

The door slammed in response, and within moments I had completed my outside work. Soon Mary and I were eating quietly, grateful for the morsels of food we had.

"I'm frightened," Mary whispered, breaking the silence.

"What for, little one? Didn't Father pronounce a blessing of protection on our home before he left this morning?"

"Yes," Mary replied hesitantly, "but Father hasn't stayed away before, and I just feel like . . . like something's going to happen."

"You are absolutely right," I replied, gathering up my half-filled milk bowl as I rose and walked to where my sacred Torah lay. "Something *is* going to happen! You are going to quietly retire to your bed; and, as I promised Father, I am going to spend the next two hours studying my Hebrew letters."

"I *can't* go to bed, Luke. Not yet. Besides, wouldn't you like me to prepare our second lamp for lighting?"

But I didn't hear my younger sister, at least not consciously. Instead, I was methodically inscribing letters in the dirt floor, my mind absorbed in the learning of the Hebraic letters as they surfaced on the scroll before me.

I had a great thirst for learning—largely because of Father's words. He had often spoken of his impressions that I would become mighty in God's hand and would likely become a rabbi. Because of his words, and because of my mother's constant example of caring for the needs of others, I have understood the need to be obedient in my quest for God.

I marveled, as I absently wrote the figures in the dirt before me, that a gift so marvelous as the Torah had been given me. I had gained a deep liking for Moses, the law-giver, who was born a full 1,570 years before this time. I have always had a deep pride for my grown-up way of thinking, and yet it was still a puzzle to me that he had been so gifted with vision as to see backward twenty-five hundred years before *his* day to record the events of Father Adam and the creation of our beautiful world.

"Luke! Luke . . ." Mary whispered urgently, breaking into my thoughts. "I think I hear something outside! It's dark out there, and I'm so frightened . . ."

"Do not fear, little one. It is only the goats."

At that moment there came a loud knock on our door, and my writing stick froze in the dirt before me. I knew of the many travelers who passed through our small village on their way to Jerusalem. Especially was the road busy since the leaders in Rome had issued a decree that all of the men return to their homes to be counted, then taxed, by the government. But still I was uneasy, as the knock came again.

Even though it was the custom of our people to trust the errands of nighttime visitors, my heart seemed to almost be in my throat as I slowly removed the latch on the door before me. When at last the door was open, I saw, standing directly before me, the dust-covered forms of a man and a woman.

"Is your father at home, my son?" the man asked, his face tired but smiling kindly.

"Uh . . . well, uh . . . no, sir, he isn't. He's . . . uh . . . he's taking his turn tending the flocks."

"And your mother?"

"Pardon me, sir, but Mother is . . . uh . . . well, she died but days ago, and . . . and my sister, Mary, and I are here . . . alone."

By then, without my knowing of it, Mary had gotten out of bed and smoothed over the covering, and was standing at my side.

Clearing his throat, the man again smiled, and asked, "Mary did I hear you say? Why, that is the most beautiful name in all of Palestine. Please," he continued, making a gesture toward his companion, "allow me to introduce my beloved, whose name is *also* Mary. My name is Joseph, and we have been traveling for so long. Mary is about to give birth to a child, and she would so appreciate a brief rest before our continuing on."

"Pl . . . please do come in," I gestured. "Father *would* count your being here a blessing, for you are strangers on the road."

The couple then entered the room, and the man called Joseph helped his companion to my sister's bed. Once there, the woman named Mary slowly removed her slippers, lifted her feet, and placed her head on the mat. It was clear to me that she was in great discomfort, for the expression in her face changed almost immediately from a very gentle smile to a look of great pain.

"Uh, did the two of you travel alone, sir? I mean, have you been traveling on foot or on beast?"

"How thoughtful of you to ask, young Luke. We do have a donkey, and I took the liberty to tether him next to your goats."

"Luke," my sister blurted, "perhaps you could go and feed the donkey, and I'll serve our guests the rest of our milk and bread."

Taken aback by the unusually adult-like words of my little sister, I simply nodded and retreated from the room. I returned moments later to find her visiting at the table with the man named Joseph. The travelers were both finishing their meager and hastily prepared meal, and my little sister's eyes were more lit up than I had seen them since before Mother's untimely passing.

"Young Luke," the woman spoke softly, her voice sounding so much like Mother's voice that I had to look twice to see who had used my name. "I . . . I think it is marvelous how you are so trusted by your father. And Mary, I do thank you for the use of your bed, and for such a fine meal."

"You're as pretty as Mommy," Mary responded, looking at the woman, "and she was the prettiest person in the *whole wide world!*"

The woman named Mary smiled weakly as her husband spoke. "That is a very generous compliment, my dear. And may I be so bold as to ask you, young Luke, how it was that your beautiful mother passed away?"

"Uh . . . well, sir," I answered, my eyes welling up again with tears, "uh . . . she died while trying to bring us a new baby brother. Father gave him the name of Joshua, but he also passed away, just hours after his birth."

I glanced then toward my little sister, who was also having a hard time holding her tears.

"Come, little one," the woman named Mary whispered. "Come to my arms. I feel such a need to hold you and to sing to you."

At such an unexpected invitation, my little sister jumped up and almost ran to where the woman lay. The two of them embraced, and quietly, while she moved her hands through my sister's hair, the woman sang the same lullaby that Mother had sung to both Mary and me each night as we fell asleep.

The man named Joseph closed his eyes as his companion sang, and I could see in the dimly lit room that a tear was working its way down his dusty cheek and into his beard.

When at last his companion stopped singing, the man spoke. "So your father is a shepherd, young Luke?"

"Yes, sir! And he said that in a year or so I will be one, as well."

"My, my! Why so long from now, my son?"

"Well, sir, several mornings ago, when Father went to the pen where all of the village sheep are kept for the night, he let me call for his sheep. I made the call, just as I had heard Father do on previous mornings. But our sheep did not even hear my voice. They just continued eating and mulling with the others. Father said that they just needed time to learn my voice. He said that sheep will only follow the voice of their master.

"Father also said that it was his feeling that soon the *true* Shepherd would come, who would be the Savior of the world. He said that, just like our sheep, we must live worthy to hear *His* voice, and then to follow Him when He calls for us to do so."

"You are full of great understanding, young Luke. What happened then?"

"Why, Father called to his sheep, and they immediately left the others of the flock and followed him into the hills."

Just then the lady named Mary cleared her throat, and spoke. "Your father must be a very good teacher, young Luke. And a most righteous servant of the great Jehovah."

"Oh, he is, my lady. And he always said that our Lord would be born to one as beautiful as our mother."

"My children," the man called Joseph quietly spoke, slowly rising to his feet, "we will always remember this evening, and the true spirit of love extended to us. May the great Jehovah bestow a special blessing on you both—and on your father, who must be the finest of men. And in some way, in *His* way, I ask a blessing on your mother this night, that she and your tiny brother might be happy, and that she will know of your well-being. She is still your mother, you know, just as Joshua is your brother; and they love you both dearly."

"Thank you most kindly, sir. Father tells us the same."

"Now we must be on our way, children," the man sighed. "Come, Mary, let us hasten down into Bethlehem before it is too late."

Just then my little sister Mary ran to the woman and began to pull on her sleeve. "Can I help you? Mother *always* asked me to help her before baby Joshua was born."

"Yes, of course, my child. I've very little strength."

For several moments my mind had been racing, as I had noticed that the woman had worn no outer coat as she came to our home. "Excuse me, my lady, but I—or *we*—have a gift for you that was left by our mother, and that she would want us to give to you."

Not waiting for a reply, I walked briskly past Mary, smiling at her as our eyes met. Reaching the chest in the corner,

I opened the lid and drew into my arms my most prized possession—the warm coat that Mother had made just days before her death, from wool extracted from our sheep.

"Here, my lady, a gift from Mary and me—and from our father and . . . and our mother."

"Why, I can't—"

"My, young Luke, but aren't you full of special surprises. Do you know the value of that garment, my son?"

"Oh, yes, sir," I replied proudly. "Father has taught the value of the coat to us, especially of the white wool edge around the coat. You see, sir, we are very poor, and yet Father wanted Mother to have the very, very best wool. In the past, he has sold the white wool to the Romans. Their gold has given us many meals. But last year, during the time of shearing, Father kept the finest, whitest wool, and gave it to Mother. She then spent months cleaning, carding, and weaving it for this coat. Well do I remember how she carefully selected the grey wool that makes up the inside of the cloak so that it all matched. And well also do I recall how proud she was that she could sew a white wool border into it."

Mary, sensing my excitement, added, "And Mother said that it was important for her to finish making the coat before Joshua was born. She said that she had a feeling that it would be needed very soon."

"And there you have it," I concluded. "Father gave the coat to me, following Mother's passing, and told me that I would know when to give it to the lady of my choice."

"But, son," Joseph protested, "I'm not sure your father would approve, I . . . "

"Sir, your companion *is* the lady of my choice. She will love it, and Mary and I will always be grateful that you came to our home and rested."

"But Luke," the woman countered, "we're total strangers."

"Mother taught us that there are *no* total strangers. She said that there are just people that we have not met.

"Besides," I added, my eyes suddenly growing moist, "this is our gift for you *and* your baby. If you are warm, your baby will be warm, too. I . . . I know that Mother would want this for you."

The woman named Mary looked inquiringly at her husband, and seeing his nod of approval she reached out and silently took the coat from my hands. Drawing the white collar to her cheek, she closed her eyes, allowing tears of her own to fall freely onto the wool fabric. Seeing those tears brought a flood of emotions to my heart, as I remembered Mother's tears as she lay cradled in Father's arms, just moments before dying.

With great discomfort in my own display of emotions, I turned quickly and walked out into the night. I knew I must get control of myself, so I wiped my tear-stained cheeks as I retrieved the traveler's donkey.

I then turned the beast and led it to our front doorway. The couple, by this time, was waiting for me. The woman looked so beautiful and radiant in the light of the lamp I held in my hand. Little Mary was holding tightly to the woman's hand, her cheek pressed against the woman's arm.

"Thank you so for coming. I will always remember you."

"Thanks to *you*, my dear. You are such a beautiful girl, and if your mother were here she would tell you both that she has never loved you more than she has this night. Remember that your mother is watching over you and is eagerly awaiting the day when she can once again take you into her arms."

"And," the man named Joseph concluded, "tell your father that he has a true shepherd for a son, even at this early age."

Quietly then, the man turned the donkey around, and as one, the rested travelers continued slowly down the path before them.

PART TWO

The Knowing

After lingering for a moment, I took my little Mary's hand and motioned for her to follow me into the house. Once inside, we knelt near her bed for our evening prayers.

"Father," I said, assuming the role to lead in prayer, "we thank thee so much for this beautiful night. Bless our mother and Joshua up in heaven, and bless Father and the sheep, that they will all be safe tonight. Thank thee also for our new friends, and please bless them that they will arrive safely in Bethlehem. Bless the keepers of the gate so they will leave it open until our friends arrive."

Nudging my arm, Mary interrupted my thoughts as she whispered, "Bless the lady, Mary, so she will have a good baby."

Again I was startled by the wisdom of my younger sister. I complied with her request, then finished the prayer.

"Luke," Mary said, "Do you think we'll be in trouble?"

"I don't know, Mary, but I have not felt this good for a long time."

"She's very pretty, Luke. She looks *just like Mother*."

I didn't respond because I couldn't. Again, without my knowing why, my eyes were suddenly welling up with tears—only this time they were tears of joy.

When I didn't answer, Mary sighed. And then, climbing into bed and closing her eyes, she said, "Goodnight, Luke. I love you so very much."

"Goodnight, Mary. Love you, too."

I lay awake for a long time after that, my mind racing with many new and wondrous thoughts. I don't remember when at last I fell asleep. I only know that I was sleeping soundly when there came a loud rapping at the door.

"Luke! Luke, please open the latch."

It was Father! Never in my life had I felt such relief!

"Quick, Luke," he said, as I allowed him to enter the house. "We must make haste. Awaken little Mary. The three of us will be going, this night, down into Bethlehem."

"But Father, it is the middle of the night, the gate to the city is locked, and . . . and . . ."

"Luke," Father replied, "the God of our fathers has unlocked many gates for his people. And this night he will unlock the most glorious one of all. Now, listen closely, as I have the most wondrous news to share."

"I . . . I don't understand, Father. The flocks . . . where are the flocks?"

"The flocks are being cared for, son, by some very special friends. But there is more that I must tell you, and then we must go. Tonight I was tending the sheep, when an angel of the Lord came to us and announced that this night the Savior of the world has been born. It is the great Messiah, Luke, and we must follow a very special star to where the newborn king awaits us—for so the angel spoke."

I just sat there, *without response*, trying to comprehend what Father had said.

Before I knew what was happening, the three of us were hurrying down the beaten path into Bethlehem. The night was full of stars, and yet, as we hurried along, Father kept pointing to one that I had not seen before. It illuminated the night and seemed to be extending downward in a precise area of the city.

It was a difficult two-mile journey, and with each step I wondered just how I could tell Father about our visitors, and about giving away the coat. But I didn't know what to say, so I kept silent as we hurried along.

By the time we were well within the city walls, little Mary had awakened. She was in equal wonderment as she was jostled along in Father's traveling sling. Before long we passed the larger homes in the city and entered the poorest neighborhood. This gave me cause to wonder, for I knew that a king would only be born in the finest of homes.

I tried to catch up to Father to ask him of this puzzlement, but when I seemed to get close to him, he simply walked faster. Gasping for breath, I was startled when Father stopped abruptly, turned, and slowly made his way down a small dirt path.

A crowd had gathered, again to my surprise, at the entry of a small, dimly lit animal stable. Before I could ask Father what was happening, he lowered little Mary to the ground, turned to me, and whispered, "The angel told us that the Christ Child would be born in a manger, in a lowly stable. Quiet now, children. We will soon have our turn."

The next few moments of my life were filled with great anxiety and excitement, as the hushed words spoken by others were so urgent. I was marveling at my unusual feelings when I felt a soft yet powerful hand press upon my shoulder.

"Young Luke," a voice whispered. "My, but you do get around."

Looking up, I found myself gazing into the kind and gentle eyes of the man named Joseph, who had stopped at our home earlier that evening.

"Uh . . . er . . . good evening, sir. I didn't expect to see you here, to see . . . uh . . . to pay homage to the Christ Child."

"It is my blessing also, young Luke—in the most wondrous manner. Now, could this be your father, the shepherd?"

Turning again to face Father, I nodded silently as the two men grasped each other's arms in greeting. Then little Mary, too, saw the man Joseph and smiled sheepishly.

"My name is Joseph," the man said, "and you, sir, must be the proud father of these two beautiful children. I'm so pleased to greet you here this night and to again enjoy the companionship of young Luke and little Mary."

"But . . . I'm afraid I don't understand," Father stammered. "Have we met before?"

"No, that we have not. But my wife and I stopped at your home earlier, and although you were tending your sheep, your children were unusually kind to my Mary and me."

"Your . . . *your* Mary?" asked Father.

"Yes, my beautiful, cherished Mary."

Without my realizing it, the crowd ahead of us had parted, and there, lying directly before us, was the lady Mary and a small baby that looked ever so much like our Joshua. And beneath the baby, protecting him from the straw of the manger, was Mother's cloak!

"Why, young Luke, and my little Mary, thank you so much for coming to see us this night. Could this be your father?"

As my mind reeled with the growing realization of what was transpiring at that moment, my father graciously bowed and introduced himself. He then nudged us forward, eager that we see the new baby—the baby that was introduced by his mother as Jesus of Nazareth, Savior of the world.

"Your baby is the *Christ Child?*" I asked, almost choking on my words.

"Yes, young Luke, and he has safely arrived because of the comfort your gift brought."

"Father," little Mary said, "look at Mother's coat in the manger. Luke gave it to her at our home, so that she could keep warm."

Before either Father or I could respond, the man Joseph softly spoke.

"My friend, your kind son, Luke, gave the coat to Mary, not knowing who we were. This gift, the *first gift*, was not given to a king. It was given to an unknown traveler, for her comfort, and for the well-being of her child. I know, young Luke," he said, turning to me, "that giving this gift was very hard for you because it reminds you of your mother and was made by her hands."

"Your gift," Mary added, "this beautiful coat, shall be cherished by us always. And when our little baby Jesus grows into a young man of your age, I shall tell him of you, and of little Mary, and of your kindness this night. Now, come children," the lady beckoned, patting the straw next to her. "Please come and sit for a moment. Little Jesus would love for you both to hold him, if just for a moment."

Father nodded approvingly, and for the next brief minute I gazed down into the eyes of the Christ Child, he whom I would later serve, and for whom I would willingly lay down my life. Mary was also smiling, as she placed her finger inside the baby's small, beautifully-formed hand. What I didn't understand was that Mary was feeling, perhaps for the very first time, the earthly touch of our Lord and Master's hand.

Reaching out, the lady Mary beckoned for us to return the baby to her. This we did. Then, while tears streamed down Father's cheeks, the woman asked little Mary and me to lean over so that she could embrace each of us.

"Here, my beautiful children," she said, kissing us both on the forehead, "your mother would have me give you these kisses, for they are from her. And in some manner she has asked that I thank each of you, again, for being so giving, so very unselfish. God has given you each a gift this night—the gift of testimony. You will always remember this hour, and you will have the great blessing of sharing it with others as you teach them of Jesus."

Words were totally beyond my capacity to give at that time, as they were for Father and little Mary. So, again bowing respectfully, we bade the couple farewell and departed into the night—a night that would forever be a beacon of light in our eyes.